LADYBIRD BOOKS, INC.
Auburn, Maine 04210 U.S.A.
© LADYBIRD BOOKS LTD 1989
Loughborough, Leicestershire, England

Printed in England

The Teddy Bear
Who Couldn't Do
Anything

By Dina Anastasio
Illustrated by Karen Loccisano

Ladybird Books

The teddy bear rested his head on the pillow and looked at the toy shelf. The other toys didn't say hello, or smile, or even nod.

They never paid any attention to him. They thought he was just a silly old bear who didn't know how to do anything.

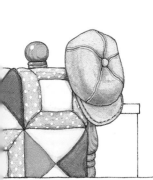

"Maybe they're right," thought the teddy bear as he looked at the other toys. "The soldier knows how to march. The ballerina knows how to dance. The monkey can play the drum. But all I can do is lie here."

Up on the shelf, the soldier was getting ready to march. He straightened his shoulders and stood tall as he stepped forward.

The teddy bear watched the shiny soldier march proudly across the shelf. He swung his arms and tapped his heels and turned smartly each time he came to the edge.

"Maybe I can stand straight and tall and march like the soldier," said the teddy bear, sitting up. "In fact, I'm *sure* I can."

The toy soldier stopped marching and stared at the bear. "What did you say?" he asked.

"Well," said the teddy bear quietly, because suddenly he wasn't so sure of himself, "I could try."

The teddy bear rolled off the bed and tried to march. But his legs were too fat and his tummy was too big....

He took three small steps and fell down.

The other toys laughed as the bear climbed back onto the bed.

Then the ballerina began to dance. Around and around she twirled.

The teddy bear tried to dance like the ballerina, but he was much too clumsy....

He fell down with a thud, and felt very foolish indeed.

"There must be something I can do," the teddy bear thought as he pulled himself back onto the bed. But as hard as he tried, he couldn't think of a single thing.

Just then, the monkey stepped forward and started to play his drum. "Tap tap," went the drum. "Tap tap tap tap tap."

The teddy bear sat up and listened. "I can do that," he said. "I can make a drumming sound like that."

The teddy bear went to the toybox and pulled out two drumsticks. Then he closed the lid and wrapped his paws around the sticks.

"Tap tap," went the drumsticks on the toybox cover.

The teddy bear smiled. At last he'd found something he could do.

But the sticks slid out of his big, fat paws and fell to the floor.

The teddy bear shook his head and sat down in the corner. "It's no use," he sighed. "I guess I really can't do anything special."

The teddy bear sat in the corner for a long time while the other toys marched and played and danced....

Then he got back into bed and slid way down beneath the covers.

When the sun set and the room grew dark, the little soldier led the ballerina and the monkey back to their places on the shelf. Soon it would be time for the boy to come into the room.

At last the boy turned on the light. He walked over to the toy shelf.

The soldier stood tall and proud.
The monkey held his drumsticks tightly.
The ballerina was on her toes, ready to dance.

But the boy shook his head.

He walked over to the bed and looked on his pillow. Then he looked under his bed.

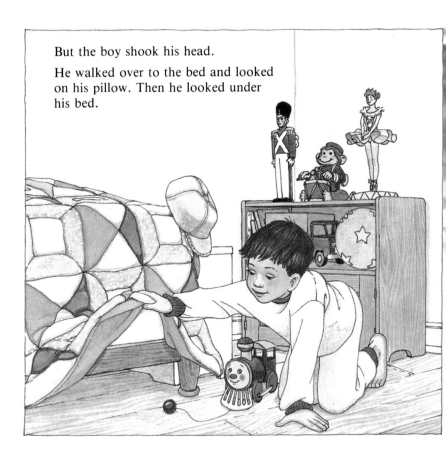

The boy's face grew worried and sad. Finally he got into bed. But he couldn't fall asleep. Something was wrong.

And then the boy's toe felt something—something soft and round and fat and nice. He reached down, deep under the covers, and found...his teddy bear.

The boy hugged the bear and was happy.

And the bear who couldn't do anything but hug was happy, too.